LOST IN THE BERMUDA TRIANGLE

The weather was perfect. A beautiful sunny day. How could the planes be lost?

"Take a bearing due West," the radio operator told the pilot.

"I can't be sure which way is West. Everything's going wrong . . . strange . . . I can't be sure of *anything*."

All the men in the radio tower stopped working. They crowded around the radio. Frowning, they listened to the pilot's voice.

"I think we must be about 225 miles Northeast of you . . ." Static cut out his voice. Then he came through again. More static. He could hardly be heard. "We're completely lost!"

The radio went dead.

It never came back to life . . .

Bantam Books in the Triumph Series
Ask your bookseller for the books you have missed

THE BERMUDA TRIANGLE AND OTHER
    MYSTERIES OF NATURE   by Edward F. Dolan
CUTTING A RECORD IN NASHVILLE
    by Lani van Ryzin
THE DISCO KID   by Curtis Gathje
THE HITCHHIKERS   by Paul Thompson
INCREDIBLE CRIMES   by Linda Atkinson
ONE DARK NIGHT   by Wallace White
PSYCHIC STORIES STRANGE BUT TRUE
    by Linda Atkinson
ROCK FEVER   by Ellen Rabinowich

THE BERMUDA TRIANGLE AND OTHER MYSTERIES OF NATURE

BY EDWARD F. DOLAN, JR.

A Triumph Book

BANTAM BOOKS
Toronto / New York / London / Sydney

THE BERMUDA TRIANGLE AND OTHER MYSTERIES OF NATURE
A Bantam Book / published by arrangement with
Franklin Watts

PRINTING HISTORY
Franklin Watts edition published Spring 1980
4 printings through December 1980
Bantam edition / October 1981

Photographs courtesy of: U.S. Navy: pp. 7; United Press International:
pp. 19, 42 (U.S. Navy Photo via UPI) 76; National Oceanic and At-
mospheric Administration: pp. 26; U.S. Air Force: pp. 51; The London
Times: pp. 62, 71.
Map on page 10 courtesy Vantage Art, Inc.

ISBN 0-553-14824-9

Published simultaneously in the United States and Canada

Bantam Books are published by Bantam Books, Inc. Its trade-
mark, consisting of the words "Bantam Books" and the por-
trayal of a bantam, is Registered in U.S. Patent and Trademark
Office and in other countries. Marca Registrada. Bantam
Books, Inc., 666 Fifth Avenue, New York, New York 10103.

PRINTED IN THE UNITED STATES OF AMERICA

0 9 8 7 6 5 4 3 2 1

Contents

PART ONE:
THE BERMUDA TRIANGLE

Chapter One
Lost at Sea
5

Chapter Two
Mysteries
14

Chapter Three
Trying to Solve the Mysteries
23

Contents

PART TWO:
UFOs

Chapter Four
Puzzles in the Sky
33

Chapter Five
Checking on the Puzzles
40

Chapter Six
From Other Worlds?
48

PART THREE:
THE ABOMINABLE SNOWCREATURE

Chapter Seven
Creatures in the Snow
59

Chapter Eight
Tracking the Snowcreature
67

Chapter Nine
The Mystery Goes On
75

Index
83

*Nature is full of strange mysteries
of the sea, the sky, and the land.
In this book are three of the greatest
of all these mysteries.*

*The first is about the sea and
the Bermuda Triangle.*

*The second looks at the sky and
at the UFOs that have been seen there.*

*The third turns to the land and to a
strange creature that may inhabit it—
the Abominable Snowcreature.*

PART ONE

THE BERMUDA TRIANGLE

Chapter One
Lost at Sea

Suddenly, the radio came alive. A voice crackled.

"Calling tower! Calling tower! This is an emergency!"

The tower radio operator leaned forward. He was at the Navy air base at Fort Lauderdale, Florida. He knew that voice. It belonged to a good pilot, Lieutenant Charles Taylor.

The voice crackled again. "I think we're off course. . . . I can't see land."

The radio operator grabbed his mike. "What is your position?"

"I'm not sure. We seem to be lost."

Lost? Impossible! Taylor was in command of five Avenger torpedo bombers. They had taken off only two hours ago for a short training flight out over the Atlantic Ocean. The weather was perfect. A beautiful sunny day. How could they be lost?

"Take a bearing due west," the radio operator said.

"I can't be sure which way is west. Everything's going wrong . . . strange. . . . I can't be sure of *anything*."

This was crazy. It was late afternoon. Anybody knew which way is west. You just had to look for the setting sun.

All the men in the tower stopped working. They crowded around the radio. Frowning, they listened to Taylor's voice. He radioed to the other pilots in his flight. They were confused, too. None of them knew where they were or which way to fly.

Long minutes passed. Fear grew in their voices. Soon, it was turning to panic. Then Taylor told one of the pilots, George Stivers, to take over command.

Stivers called the tower.

**Five bombers much like
those pictured here
disappeared without
a trace during a
test flight in 1945.**

"I think we must be about 225 miles [362.1 km] northeast of you. . . ." Static cut out his voice. Then he came through again. More static. He could hardly be heard. "We're completely lost!"

The radio went dead.

It never came back to life.

An officer ran to the tower phone. He called the nearby air rescue station for help. Minutes later, a Mariner flying boat roared into the air. It was a big ship—the best there was for a rescue at sea. On board were twelve highly trained men.

The Mariner headed northeast. It reached its destination in half an hour. The sun was almost down. The pilot swept low over the sea. Then he radioed the tower.

"No sign of the planes. No wreckage. Nothing. We'll continue to search. Over and out."

The radio fell silent.

And *it* never again returned to life.

Night came. The radio operator tried to contact the Mariner time and again. Not a single answer was heard. The men in the tower stared at each other. There had been five planes in trouble. Now there were six.

By now, the tower had called for more help. Coast Guard ships raced to the trouble-spot. An aircraft carrier joined them and launched its planes at dawn. Ships and planes searched the ocean for miles around.

Onshore, sailors hiked all along the Florida coast. They looked for washed-up wreckage.

The search on land and sea lasted for days. It covered thousands of square miles.

And it turned up nothing. No wreckage. No life rafts. No bodies. Not even a shred of clothing.

Six planes and their crews had vanished without a trace. Navy officers couldn't believe what had happened. One said, "It's impossible. It's as if they flew off to Mars."

And why had the torpedo bomber pilots been so confused? Lieutenant Taylor and his men were all good fliers. The weather had been fine. They should have been able to find their way home. No one could figure it out.

The disappearance took place in 1945. The planes vanished in one of the world's great mystery spots. It's located in the Atlantic Ocean just off the United States coast. Most people know it

THE BERMUDA TRIANGLE

as the Bermuda Triangle. Some call it the Devil's Triangle.

To find the Triangle on a map, you start at Norfolk, Virginia. Then, draw a line out to the Bermuda Islands. Next, take the line south to Puerto Rico. Finally, head back to the United States so that you end up at Miami, Florida.

Inside the lines is a vast triangle of ocean. It covers about 440,000 square miles (1,139,600 sq km). Hundreds of planes and ships pass through it each year. Most make the trip safely. But the Triangle has a bad name. It has swallowed up too many planes and ships.

Look at what happened just a few weeks before the six planes disappeared. Twelve Navy Hell Divers took off from Jacksonville, Florida. They were on a training flight. They swept out over the Atlantic on a clear day. No one ever saw them again. There wasn't even a radio call for help this time.

And look what happened to Dan Burack's cabin cruiser, *Witchcraft*. He and a friend took the 23-foot (7-m) boat for a short run one night in 1967. They went out just 1 mile (1.6 km) from shore. They wanted to look at the lights of Miami from the sea.

At nine o'clock, Burack radioed the Coast Guard.

"I've hit something under the water," he reported. "Everything's OK, except that my propellers are bent. I need a tow back to the port."

Burack didn't think he was in danger. The hull hadn't been damaged. Even if there had been damage, he wouldn't have been worried. The *Witchcraft* had special compartments. They would keep it from sinking. And there were life jackets on board.

A Coast Guard cutter hurried to his aid. It arrived in just fifteen minutes only to find the *Witchcraft* gone. Other ships were called. They searched the entire area. Divers went down to see if the cabin cruiser had sunk. The *Witchcraft* and its two passengers were never found.

The Bermuda Triangle has long been full of mysteries like these. More than 100 ships and planes have vanished there since 1945. Lost with them have been more than 1,000 lives.

But the mysteries did not begin in 1945. People have been aware of them since the 1800s.

At least six ships vanished in the 1800s without leaving a trace of wreckage behind. Four were American warships. One was a British training ship with 290 men aboard.

Then, more than forty ships were swallowed up between 1900 and 1945. Some were sailing ships. Some were steamers. Most were cargo vessels. One was a passenger ship. At least three aircraft disappeared before 1945.

These mysteries have puzzled the entire world. But there's something else. The Triangle hasn't just swallowed up ships and planes. There have been *other* mysteries as well.

They started in 1492.

Chapter Two
Mysteries

"Captain! Look!"

There was fear in the old sailor's voice. He yanked one hand off the ship's wheel. He pointed to the compass just in front of him.

The Captain's eyes followed the shaking finger. Then his face grew tense.

It was a beautiful day. Sunny and clear. The ship was charging along under full sail. But the *compass* . . .

Until a second ago, it had been steady. Now the needle was going mad. It was swinging wildly back and forth. It had never done this before.

The sailor's voice came close to a scream.

"The devil's got it, sir! The devil . . ."

"Be quiet! Don't talk like a fool."

"But . . ."

"Quiet, I said!"

The sailor obeyed. The Captain bent low over the compass and watched the swinging movements. It didn't make sense. But they went on and on for a very long minute. Then they stopped as suddenly as they had begun. The needle was quiet again.

The Captain let his breath go.

"It's over. Everything is all right."

"What happened, sir? What caused it?"

"I don't know," the Captain answered honestly.

The old sailor was deathly pale. He looked out at the sea. He swallowed hard.

"I don't like it here, sir. And that's the honest truth."

Nor do I, the Captain thought. This was a bad stretch of the Atlantic Ocean. It was full of strange happenings. He'd be glad to have it behind him.

His mind went back to the other afternoon. A blinding light had flashed in the sky. It was brighter than the sun and had turned into a giant ball of fire. It went streaking across the horizon. Frightened, the sailors had watched it crash into the sea.

Then there had been the night before last. The Captain had been walking the deck. He'd stopped, gasping at what he saw. It was a light glowing under the water. A whitish light. A ghostly light.

Indeed, he'd be happy to put this stretch of ocean behind him.

The Captain was Christopher Columbus. He was sailing west from Spain. In a few more weeks, he'd sight land. And he'd go down in history as the man who discovered the New World. And, as a man who had seen the mysteries of the Bermuda Triangle.

A century later, another explorer saw something just as strange. He was George Somers of England. In 1607, he sailed near this same spot. He later told a friend that he came out on deck one night. It was very dark.

"Suddenly, there was a light above me. I looked up. . . . It seemed to be a flame high in the rigging. It moved like a ghost along the ropes. Then it ran up the mainmast. It flickered for a moment. It went out, but came on again. . . . After that, it jumped from mast to mast . . . until it disappeared. . . ."

Somers thought he was seeing an evil spirit. Today, some people think it was probably "St. Elmo's fire"—an eerie light created by electricity in the air. But no one really knows.

Just as no one really knows what happened to the fishing boat *Wild Goose* in 1944. It was being towed by a ship called the *Caicos Trader*. Suddenly, something went wrong. The fishing boat pitched upwards. Then it put its nose down. Finally, it vanished beneath the water.

The crew on the *Caicos Trader* said later, "It looked as if it had been caught in a whirlpool."

They ran to the towline that stretched down to the fishing boat. Quickly, they cut the line before it pulled their own ship under. Then they stared at the empty sea in horror. There was a man aboard the *Wild Goose*.

He was Joe Talley, its captain. He'd gone to sleep in his cabin a little earlier. He snapped wide-awake as water poured over him. He grabbed a life jacket. The cabin porthole was open. He squeezed through it and swam to the surface, more than 40 feet (12.2 m) away.

On cutting the towline, the *Caicos Trader* steamed a short distance to safety. Then it came back to look for Talley. No one expected to find him. But there he was, floating in the sea and waving for help.

What had pulled his boat under? Was it a whirlpool? Or some strange force?

A strange force seemed to be at work one morning in 1967. The liner *Queen Elizabeth I* was steaming in the Triangle. Two sailors were on deck. They looked up to see a small plane flying low about 300 yards (274.3 m) away. One seaman thought that it was a Piper Comanche.

In the next instant, the men couldn't believe their eyes. The plane banked. It came straight at them.

Then . . .

It disappeared into the sea when it was still 100 yards (91.4 m) away. There was no splash. No sound. The plane just vanished.

**A reward poster for a
yacht thought to be missing
in the Bermuda Triangle.**

The seamen reported the crash to their superiors. They said that the ocean just seemed to open up and swallow the plane. But no one believed their story.

Something even stranger happened in 1935. The waters of the Triangle swallowed a ship. Then they sent it back to the surface, or so it seemed.

It all started when a freighter was sailing near the Bermuda Islands. It sighted a yacht called the *La Dahama*. No one could be seen on deck. Several crew members went aboard the yacht. They could find no sign of life. But they discovered the yacht's logbook. They brought the book back to the freighter as proof of their visit. Then they sailed away, leaving the *La Dahama* behind.

On arriving home, they heard a weird story. A passenger liner had come upon the yacht five days before the freighter had sighted it. The *La Dahama* had been sinking. Its passengers had been taken aboard the liner. Then everyone had watched as the yacht began to disappear beneath the waves.

The yacht had sunk days before the freighter sighted it. Yet the freighter's crew had its logbook as proof of their visit. It was all impossible!

But no more impossible than the story of Bruce Gernon. He was flying his Beechcraft Bonanza from the Bahama Islands to Florida in 1970. A great cloud loomed in front of him soon after takeoff. He flew above it, only to have it chase him. Then it closed around him. It was shaped like a tunnel. Some of his instruments stopped working.

Gernon flew along inside the cloud for several minutes. At last, he broke free. He looked down—and there was Miami Beach. He shook his head. The trip should have taken an hour and fifteen minutes. But he'd made it in forty-five minutes.

His plane just couldn't fly *that* fast. But it had.

These have been just a handful of the Triangle's many mysteries. Can any reasons be found for them? Or for all the disappearing ships and planes? People have been trying to find the answer for years.

There have been plenty of ideas. But no answers.

Chapter Three
Trying to Solve the Mysteries

Let's start with the ships and planes that have vanished in the Triangle.

Some scientists feel that there is really nothing mysterious about them. "Would you like to know what actually happened?" they ask. "Then just take a look at some of the physical forces in the Triangle."

First, they point to the Gulf Stream. It's a strong current that passes between the Bahama Islands and Florida. It moves along at more than four knots.

"Suppose a plane crashes," the scientists say. "Or a small ship hits a reef and sinks. Of course, the searchers can't find any wreckage. The current has carried everything away by the time they get there."

But the searchers know how the current works. And so they always check it. Very closely. But they still can't find the ships and planes. Why?

The scientists believe that one answer can be found on the sea bottom. The bottom is covered in many places with quicksand. The wreckage is carried away by the current and dumped in some distant spot. It sinks out of sight in the quicksand.

"And there's something else," one scientist explains. "Much of the sea bottom is made up of limestone mountains. There are caves cutting into these mountains everywhere. A strong current flows in the caves. It's strong enough to pull in small ships and planes that have sunk. Then they remain hidden there."

A few years ago, a diver was exploring one of the caves. He came upon a fishing boat wedged in between the rocks. The boat was 80 feet (24.4 m) below the surface.

The currents in the caves are also strong enough to cause whirlpools up on the surface. The whirlpools can trap passing boats and pull them under. Joe Talley's *Wild Goose* may have been caught in such a whirlpool.

There are also tidal waves in the Triangle. They're often caused by undersea earthquakes. Some rise over 200 feet (60.6 m) high. They can swamp a good-sized ship. Or roll it over. Or break it into pieces that are carried away either to the quicksand or to the caves.

Remember the *La Dahama?* Some people believe that a rising tidal wave brought it back to the surface.

Then there are waterspouts. These are tornadoes at sea. Great funnels of water swirl into the sky when the winds collide. They can tear a small or medium-sized ship apart. The same goes for aircraft that flies into them.

The winds in the Triangle can cause the same kind of trouble. They're like the winds all over the world. They blow in different directions at different altitudes. A plane can be sent bouncing when a wind hits it from a new direction.

Now suppose the wind at a certain altitude is very strong. And suppose you're flying at great speed. Without warning, you smash into the wind.

**Waterspouts have been blamed
by some people as the source
of many mysterious occurrences
in the Bermuda Triangle.**

Your plane may not just bounce. It may well be ripped to pieces, even if it's a pretty large one.

Along with everything else, the planes and ships are often hit by storms. But storms don't seem to play a great part in the Bermuda Triangle mysteries. Most of the ships and planes have vanished in good weather, on clear, sunny days.

All these physical forces—from quicksand to storms—are possible reasons for the disappearances. But no one knows for sure if they are really behind the trouble. Not even scientists.

Other reasons have been given for the disappearances. Some of them can stagger the imagination. One man believes that there are "openings" in the air of the Triangle. They are invisible doorways to another world. This world, he believes, is the exact opposite of ours. It is a world of "antimatter." If you come near one of the openings, you're pulled into this strange world, never to be seen again.

Is there any truth to this man's belief? Who can say?

Now let's turn to the other kinds of mysteries. What about the compass that went wild as Columbus watched? What about Lieutenant Taylor in 1945? Why did he lose his sense of direction?

The Triangle is full of stories like these. Many compasses have gone wild. Radios have failed. The batteries on ships have suddenly gone dead. And there have been many pilots just as confused as Lieutenant Taylor.

In 1962 a private plane was approaching one of the Bahama Islands. The day was sunny. The pilot should have been able to see the island. But he kept asking the airport tower for directions. He was completely lost. He disappeared out over the sea and was never found.

Many scientists think that all the trouble is caused by strange magnetic forces. These forces knock out electrical equipment and cause pilots to lose their sense of direction. They may even cause mysterious clouds to form, like the one that caught Bruce Gernon's plane.

One scientist says, "Matter from outer space may have landed in the Triangle long ago. It upset the earth's magnetism in that area."

The Triangle isn't the only place in the world with magnetic problems. There are nine other areas where things just as strange happen to electrical equipment. They're all triangular in shape and are all located near the equator. One is in the Pacific Ocean. Another is in the Indian Ocean. And one is in Afghanistan.

Were all these areas hit by matter from outer space? Or is the world built in some strange way near the equator?

The magnetic forces in the Triangle may cause an extra problem. They may throw time out of kilter. Remember how Bruce Gernon reached Miami far ahead of schedule when he was caught in that mysterious cloud?

Something similar happened to an airliner in the 1960s. It was heading toward the Miami airport from the sea. Suddenly, it disappeared from the radar screen in the tower. The blip was gone for ten minutes. Then it appeared again. A few moments later, the airliner flew in and landed.

The plane's crew was surprised to learn that they had been off the radar screen for ten minutes. Nothing strange had happened to them during that time. Then they looked at their watches and were even more surprised.

All the watches were exactly ten minutes behind time!

There is another idea that many people have, including a number of scientists. They think it answers all the mysteries in the Triangle.

They believe that the Triangle is used as a "collecting station" by visitors from outer space. Spaceships from other planets arrive regularly. They cause the magnetic problems and the disappearances. They take our people, planes, and ships aboard and carry them home for study.

How much truth is there in this idea and in all the others? At present, no one can say. But, one day, scientists may find out. Then we'll know the answers.

But, until then, the Bermuda Triangle will remain one of the world's great mysteries.

PART TWO

UFOs

Chapter Four

Puzzles
in the Sky

The pilot blinked. Then he stared. He could hardly believe what he was seeing as he flew his private plane above the state of Washington. There were nine strange objects flying in the distance. They weren't planes. At least, not any types of planes that he had ever seen.

They were shaped like discs. Like . . .

"Saucers."

That was the word businessman Kenneth Arnold used when he landed. He told some newspaper reporters what he had seen. He said that the discs had been a shiny silver. They had been flying at great speed near Mount Rainier in a triangular formation.

"They looked like saucers skipping over the water," Arnold said.

The date was June 24, 1947. The newsmen took the word "saucers" and turned it into "flying saucers." Arnold's story made headlines all over the world. People everywhere were fascinated by it. They wondered what he had actually seen.

"Maybe they were spaceships from another planet," some said.

"Or new warplanes that the United States has developed."

"Or that some other country has developed."

No one knew. But the term "flying saucers" quickly became part of our language. It's still in the language. But, more often, we now use a better term—UFOs. It stands for *unidentified flying objects*.

An unidentified flying object is any mysterious thing that appears in the sky. It may be seen by the eye. Or it may be picked up on a radar screen. At the time it is being seen, no one can say for sure what is causing it. Sometimes, the cause is learned later. Sometimes not.

When Kenneth Arnold's story first came out,

many people thought that UFOs were something new. Since then, we've learned differently. UFOs are very old. In fact, they've been sighted since the earliest times.

They may have been seen in China 45,000 years ago. Great stone carvings have been found there. They show men standing on cylindrical objects in the sky. Perhaps an artist made these carvings from his imagination. Or perhaps the early Chinese did see some strange "ships" in the sky.

The Bible tells of another early sighting. The prophet Ezekiel saw a fiery object in 532 B.C. It flew out of a whirlwind. It landed near a river in the country of Chaldea in the Middle East. The object seemed to be made up of four pillars. Two wings came from each pillar. There was a circular opening at the base of each pillar from which smoke poured out. The wings moved and sounded like rushing water.

In nearby Egypt, something strange was seen around 1500 B.C. A "circle of fire" shot out of the sky. It terrified the people who saw it. It gave off a foul smell. After a while it was joined by other fiery circles. They glowed brighter than the sun as they hovered overhead. Then they flew off to the south.

Sightings such as these were made throughout the following centuries. Objects were seen in all parts of the world.

For instance, some farmers in Japan said that they glimpsed a silvery disc. It swept down close to the ground. The year was A.D. 1133.

A strange object flew over the French town of Arras about 300 years later, in 1461. It looked like a giant boat. Flames were shooting from it.

One night in 1868, several British astronomers were surprised. They saw a shiny thing fly past their telescope. The object was disc-shaped. As they watched, it flew in several different directions. Then it vanished into the darkness.

An astronomer in Mexico was just as surprised in 1883. A fleet of discs flashed across the moon. He counted them. They numbered 243.

One of the strangest sightings occurred one night in 1897 in the United States. A Kansas farmer named Alexander Hamilton awoke to the sound of his cows mooing. They seemed to be frightened. He hurried outside to see what the trouble was. He fell back in fear and amazement.

There was a giant airship of some sort just above his cow corral. He had never seen anything like it in his life.

Hamilton yelled for his son and a hired hand. They all grabbed axes and ran toward the corral. The ship was hovering about 30 feet (9.1 m) above the ground. They stopped a short distance from it.

"The thing was shaped like a cigar," Hamilton said later. "It was maybe 300 feet [91.4 m] long. It seemed to be a darkish red."

The farmer made out some sort of control cabin underneath the ship. It was made of glass or some other clear substance. A light glowed inside. There were six figures at the controls.

Hamilton later said they were "the strangest things I ever saw. They were all jabbering together. But we couldn't understand a word they said."

The three men stood gaping at the craft. Then the figures inside saw them. Instantly, an engine whirred. A big turbine wheel near the control cabin began to turn. The ship rose slowly to a height of about 300 feet (91.4 m).

It was then that Hamilton saw one of his heifers over by the corral fence. She was bawling with fear. A cable hung down from the ship and was wrapped around her. It pulled her up to the control cabin. She disappeared inside. The ship flew off to the north.

Hamilton found the body of the heifer the next day in a field about 3 miles (4.8 km) from his farm. The animal had been killed. The ground all around was soft and muddy. But there were no footprints.

The farmer never forgot the strange ship and its jabbering crew. They gave him nightmares for years to come.

UFO sightings continued into our present century. Many were made during World War II. Objects were glimpsed over Germany, France, Turkey, and Greece. In 1944, a United States fighter pilot ran into a string of them over France. Ten "balls of fire" whizzed past him.

Often, the sightings have come in "waves." No one will see a thing for months. Or years. Then, suddenly, people will make one sighting after another.

This happened in the United States in 1897. People in Illinois, Missouri, and Texas all sighted UFOs. And don't forget farmer Hamilton in Kansas. His bad dreams began that year.

There was a wave of sightings in parts of Europe in 1946. And another wave in the United States during 1947, the year that Kenneth Arnold glimpsed those nine "saucers." The 1950s saw waves all over the world. The busiest year was 1952 when people reported more than 1,500 sightings.

What have all the people actually seen? Have they seen spaceships? Or lights reflected against the night sky? Or have they just been imagining things?

There's no way of telling what the people of times past really saw. But work has been done to find out what the people of our day have seen. And are still seeing.

Chapter Five
Checking
on the Puzzles

The year was 1947. News of flying saucers filled the newspapers. Kenneth Arnold had seen them. Then other people had glimpsed all sorts of objects in the sky. The United States was having a "wave" of sightings.

Most Americans thought it was all something new. They hadn't heard of the sightings in the past. They were fascinated. Many were frightened as well. Everyone wondered if the country was being visited by creatures from outer space.

The government in Washington, D.C., was worried. Did the saucers indeed come from outer space? Were they a threat to the nation? Or were there other causes for the sightings?

The Air Force was ordered to find out. It did so by starting a study called *Project Blue Book*.

Soon after the study began, the Air Force dropped the term "flying saucers." This was done because so many of the things sighted were not disc-shaped. Some resembled cigars. Some looked like needles. Some were stabs of light. Some were just blips on radar screens. The term "unidentified flying objects," or UFOs, was born.

Project Blue Book lasted for twenty-two years. It studied more than 12,000 reports of sightings. It sent out investigators to learn what the people had actually seen. The investigators found the causes behind most of the sightings. They had nothing to do with spaceships. Or with visitors from other planets.

First, nature itself had fooled many of the people. Some UFOs turned out to be strangely shaped clouds. Others proved to be flashes or bolts of lightning. Still others were found to be meteors that had streaked across the heavens.

Next, many sightings were of aircraft. A person might see the lights of a plane at night and not know what they were. Some people

Flying saucers? No, they're just saucer-shaped clouds that appeared one evening over a town in southern France.

thought they were seeing spaceships when they were really looking at experimental aircraft out on test runs.

Often, the trails of smoke left by large planes were mistaken for UFOs.

Sometimes, lights on the ground were at fault. One man reported seeing a weird light bouncing across the night sky. It was actually the beam of a searchlight. Another man was sure that he had seen several shiny discs. They flew in front of a low cloud. Investigators showed him that they had been the reflections of car head-lights.

One "lights case" had a funny ending. A passenger on a plane reported a UFO one night. He'd seen a blinking light just outside his window. It had moved right along with the plane.

Investigators checked the window. It was made up of two panes of glass. The panes were side by side with a narrow airspace in between. The "UFO" was a firefly that had somehow got into the airspace.

Weather balloons caused many a sighting. In

fact, *Project Blue Book* found that weather balloons were behind almost 25 percent of all the sightings. They fooled practically everyone. Even very experienced fliers.

One night, a Navy pilot was flying above the Caribbean Sea. He radioed his base.

"I've got visual contact with something. It's an orange light. I'm going in for a closer look."

He dove toward the object, only to have it run from him. He gave chase. The thing disappeared into a cloud for a while. It dipped down close to the sea. Then it shot skyward again. The pilot later learned that he'd been chasing a weather balloon. It hadn't been running from him. Some heavy air currents had been bouncing it around.

Quite a number of sightings proved to be hoaxes. A student once glued a penny to the window in his room. Then he stood across the room and photographed the window.

In the picture, the penny seemed to be a disc floating above the trees outside. The student told the newspapers it was a flying object. His trick photography was soon uncovered.

Project Blue Book also uncovered something else. Many people had only imagined seeing UFOs. They honestly *believed* they had seen something. But, actually, nothing had been in the sky. The flying objects were "all in their heads."

Many doctors felt that "waves" of sightings were also a result of active imaginations. A person would see an object, or think that he or she did. After it was reported in the newspapers, other people would begin sighting objects like it.

Doctors said that there was yet another reason why people might imagine seeing UFOs. One doctor explained it this way:

"We live in troubled times. Some people wish that someone would come in and solve the world's problems. Someone who is superior to us. Someone from an advanced planet. That wish can cause a person to see a spaceship in the sky. He's just hoping that help is coming at last."

Overactive imaginations seemed to play a great part in some of the most fascinating UFO reports. These were the reports of people who said they met "crew members" in the UFOs.

One man told of meeting crew members from

a ship that came from the planet Venus. He drew several pictures of them. The pictures showed them to have long hair. They were wearing short jackets and ski pants.

A woman claimed that she met some outer space visitors who were angels. They were standing by to prevent an atomic war on earth. She claims she went for a short ride in their ship.

Some meetings were hoaxes. A man reported that his truck ran over a space creature. He gave the police a small body as proof. The body measured about 20 inches (50.8 cm) long. It was shriveled up. It was hairless and looked a little like a man.

A medical examination showed the "space-creature" to be a monkey. The animal's hair had been shaved off. Its tail had been cut off.

Project Blue Book felt that most reports of space visitors were works of the imagination. And many came from people who were known to be mentally unbalanced. But there were some reports that mystified everyone. There seemed to be some truth in them.

A very famous one came from Mr. and Mrs.

Barney Hill of New Hampshire. A giant disc flew over their car one night. All of a sudden, they lost consciousness. When they came to, they could not remember what had happened to them.

A doctor placed the couple under hypnosis. They told of being taken aboard the disc. Some creatures with great eyes had then examined them.

Did all this really happen? Or did the Hills just believe that it had? Could they have believed it so deeply that they both told the same story under hypnosis? To this day, no one really knows.

Project Blue Book investigated UFO sightings throughout the 1950s and 1960s. Several scientific groups also made studies. They all agreed with the Air Force that most of the sightings had not been of actual spaceships. They had been things right here on Earth. The Air Force ended *Project Blue Book* in 1970.

But many of the sightings had not been solved. They remained a mystery. No earthly reasons had been found for the objects. They didn't seem to be cloud formations. Or reflected lights. Or weather balloons.

Then what were they?

Chapter Six

From Other Worlds?

There have been hundreds of unsolved sightings in recent years. They've been reported from practically every part of the world.

Let's start with an airliner in 1948. It was flying from Hong Kong to Vietnam. Suddenly, the passengers and crew saw an object in the distance. They thought it looked like a giant silverfish. The thing was moving at a tremendous speed, yet no smoke or flames came from it. Without slowing down, it made a sharp turn and disappeared into a cloud.

In 1951, a family was driving near a lake in Switzerland. A disc appeared above the lake. It flew along in a series of stops-and-starts. It would remain motionless for a moment, then jump ahead. Once, it turned itself upside down. Then it shot straight up and vanished. Not once did it make a sound.

A number of people in Korea never forgot what they saw the following year. A large object shaped like a wheel appeared in the sky. It gave off an orange light. Blue flames came from its edges. The startled Koreans watched it for several minutes before it flew off.

A French businessman was just as startled in 1954. He was standing outside his house late one night. A pale light suddenly filled the sky. He looked up to see a strange shape above the river nearby.

"It looked like a huge cigar standing on end," he said later. He guessed that it was about 300 feet (91.4 m) long.

As he watched, the bottom of the object opened. Five discs dropped from the opening, one by one. They fell toward the river. But they stopped before hitting the water. They swayed for a moment, then flew off at great speeds. Each was surrounded by a halo of light. After the discs flew off, the "mother ship" faded into the darkness.

This sighting took place in a town called Vernon. It lasted for about forty-five minutes. The cigar and the discs were also seen by two police officers and an engineer.

Another night sighting was reported six years later. Two California highway police officers glimpsed a huge object falling from the sky. They thought it was an airliner about to crash. But, when it was 100 feet (30.5 m) from the ground, it shot high in the air again. It then flew in several different directions. The police officers followed it for two hours before it finally vanished.

One afternoon in 1963, several people saw a disc land in a field near Epping, England. One man later reported, "I'd say it was about 8 feet [2.4 m] long and 3 feet [.9 m] high." The disc remained on the ground for a little while. Then it took off. It disappeared behind some trees. No one ever saw it again.

People went to the spot where the thing had landed. It seemed as if a great weight had been

**New or experimental aircraft
such as this jet
are often mistaken for
unidentified flying objects.**

there. A circle of grass had been flattened. The earth was pushed down.

One of the most famous of all sightings took place near Exeter, New Hampshire. The year was 1965. At two o'clock in the morning, a police officer saw a giant disc skim over the trees. It glowed with brilliant lights and was about 100 feet (30.5 m) in diameter. The whole thing moved along without a sound. It swept by so low that the police officer threw himself to the ground. He pulled out his revolver but did not fire.

The object was also seen by another police officer and a naval officer. In the next few days, UFOs were reported all through the area. Some were seen hovering above utility lines as if they drew electricity from them. Then there was a major power failure. It blacked out parts of New Hampshire and parts of the four surrounding states.

A very recent sighting was made over the country of Iran. A fighter pilot spotted a glowing disc. He moved his plane in for a closer look. Suddenly, the disc released a small object. The object headed straight for the plane. The pilot got ready to fire a missile at it. But his control panel went dead and he could do nothing.

The pilot swung away to avoid a collision. At that moment, the object turned and went back to its "mother ship." The two of them then flew off.

What caused these unsolved sightings? And all the other unsolved ones that have been made through the years? Different scientists have different views.

Some believe that we're being visited by spaceships from other "worlds." They point out that the universe contains billions of stars with planets around them. Surely, many of the planets have life on them, perhaps even civilizations more advanced than ours. Some of those civilizations are probably reaching out for a look at Earth.

Most scientists, however, don't agree with this view. They feel that there probably is life on planets throughout the universe. But it seems unlikely that ships could travel from them to Earth. First, too much energy would be needed.

One scientist puts it this way:

"Suppose you build a rocket that can move at seven-tenths the speed of light. Suppose you put twelve men on board. You send them to our nearest star and back. Do you know how much electricity would be needed for the trip? Five hundred thousand times the amount that the United States puts out each year."

Then there's the matter of distance. Our nearest star is 4.3 light-years away. A light-year is the distance that light can travel in twelve months at 186,000 miles (296,000 km) a second. And that's the *nearest* star. Others are thousands and even millions of light-years away. It would take ships an impossible amount of time to get here.

But what about the planets in our own solar system? Could ships be coming from them? It doesn't seem likely.

The planets Pluto, Jupiter, Saturn, Uranus, and Neptune all seem too cold for life as we know it. Mercury and Venus are too hot. Mars may support life. But it's probably some form of plant life. We've sent space probes to Mars. They've found no evidence that Mars has life that is able to launch a spaceship toward Earth.

Then what's behind the unsolved sightings? Most scientists believe that they're the same as all the other sightings and are caused by earthly forces. Things from experimental aircraft to lights and gases. It's just that the causes haven't yet been found.

But there *are* scientists who believe in spaceships. They argue that inhabitants on other planets may know how to travel faster than we think possible. And they point to governments. They have kept many UFO sightings a secret. Why? They may think that the people will be too frightened by what they have learned.

Who is right?

Who is wrong?

Someday, we may find out. Then UFOs will no longer be one of nature's great mysteries.

PART THREE

THE ABOMINABLE SNOWCREATURE

Chapter Seven

Creatures in the Snow

The two creatures appeared suddenly. They stood for a moment in the snow high on the mountainside.

They seemed to be part human and part animal. They stood erect like humans. But they wore no clothing. And they were covered from head to foot with thick, reddish-brown hair.

"Look!"

The cry came from a Norwegian mountain climber just below them. The men with him stopped climbing. They stared upward. Astonishment showed in their faces. Then fear.

"What are they?"

No one had a chance to answer. With great

strides, the creatures moved toward the men. One climber grabbed a rope. He made it into a lasso. He tried to toss it over the first of the creatures. But the thing grabbed him. It bit his arm and threw him to the ground.

Another climber brought out a rifle. He fired it into the air. Instantly, the creatures turned and headed back up the mountainside. They disappeared behind some rocks and were gone.

All this happened in 1948 while the Norwegians were hiking through a mountain pass in Nepal. When they returned to civilization, they told their story to the newspapers.

But there was a problem. The Norwegians had brought back no proof of the meeting. No photographs. No tufts of reddish-brown hair. And no bodies. They had fired the rifle into the air but never *at* the creatures. Though frightened, the climbers hadn't wanted to hurt them.

And so not everyone believed the story. Some people thought that the Norwegians had been "seeing things." After all, the men had been in the high, thin air for a long time. Maybe it had affected their minds.

But other people believed the story. They were sure that the climbers had come face-to-face with one of nature's great mysteries. The Norwegians had seen the beast that is known all across the world as the Abominable Snowcreature.

And they had seen not just one but two!

The mystery of the Abominable Snowcreature isn't just a great one. It's also a very old one. It started centuries ago in Nepal, the small country that lies between India and Tibet. Nepal is crossed by the great Himalaya Mountains. Crowning them all is Mount Everest, with the highest peak in the world. Everest stands on the border of Tibet. It towers 29,000 feet (8,800 m) above sea level.

Among the people of Nepal are the Sherpas. Living high in the mountains, they raise a few animals and crops. And they serve as guides for the adventurers who come to scale the Himalayas. These rugged, brown-faced people seem to be the ones who gave birth to the mystery of the Snowcreature.

They claim that they've been seeing it for

**Strange footprints found in
the Himalaya Mountains
thought to belong to a Yeti.**

generations. Or sighting its tracks in the snow. Or hearing its chilling cry. The cry sounds like a cross between a whistle and a howl.

The Sherpas claim that the Snowcreature is much like a human being. It walks upright on two legs. It swings its arms and uses its hands to grab things. Sometimes, it is about the size of a large person—from 6 to 8 feet (1.8 to 2.4 m) tall. Sometimes, it looms a giant 10 to 15 feet (3.0 to 4.6 m) high. And sometimes it is only about 5 feet (1.5 m) tall—the height of a youngster.

These different heights have caused some Sherpas to wonder. Perhaps there are different kinds of Snowcreatures. Maybe three kinds. The Sherpas say that the largest Snowcreatures are seen only high in the mountains—at elevations over 13,000 feet (42,640 km). The smaller ones are seen lower down the slopes.

No matter what its size, the Snowcreature is always covered with hair. It is thick and matted. Most often, it is reddish or brown. Some Sherpas report that they've seen, or heard about, Snowcreatures with white, gray, or black hair.

The Snowcreature has a large head. It's

shaped like a dome and comes to a point at the top. Long hair falls about the face. The face itself is something like a human's. But it's a terrible thing to see. The mouth is very wide. The teeth are large and may even be fangs. The eyes are great and sunken. Some say they glow like red coals.

Many Sherpas are especially afraid of the eyes. They believe that death will come if you look into them.

There's a wild story among the Sherpas about the Snowcreature's feet. The feet are said to be pointing backwards. This enables the creature to run away while keeping an eye on whoever is chasing it.

Long ago, the Sherpas gave the Snowcreature a name—Yeti. It has several meanings in their language. It can mean "the creature who lives in high places." Or "the creature who lives among the rocks." Or "the magical one." Or "the creature who eats anything."

Where did the name "Abominable Snowcreature" come from? The newspapers of the Western world dreamed it up when the first stories of the Yeti made their way out of Nepal some years ago.

The tales of the Yeti are many among the Sherpas. There are stories of Snowcreatures creeping into villages and stealing away people and animals for food. There are stories of finding large tracks in the snow. Tracks that could be made only by a giant. Sherpan children are warned to be good, or the Yeti will come and get them.

The most famous of all Sherpas is Tenzing Norgay. In 1953, he and Sir Edmund Hillary of New Zealand became the first men ever to reach the top of Mount Everest. Tenzing has never seen a Snowcreature. But he says his father has.

Tenzing says that his father was out hiking one day when he came upon a Yeti. It was feeding on a goat that it had killed. The hairy creature straightened its body. With a howl, it came running at the man. Tenzing's father turned and fled down the mountainside. The Snowcreature never caught up with him. It couldn't move quickly while going downhill.

Was Tenzing's father telling the truth? Did he really meet a Yeti? Are all Sherpas telling the truth when they talk about these strange beasts?

Tenzing answers by saying that his father never lies.

But this isn't enough for many people across the world. They believe there is no such thing as an Abominable Snowcreature. First, they say no one has ever proved that the creature actually exists. Like the Norwegian climbers, no one has even taken a picture of it.

Next, they say that the Sherpas are a primitive people, full of the superstitions and fears of primitive people everywhere. They believe the Sherpas aren't lying. They've probably seen something. But most people think it's probably some kind of animal. Perhaps a bear or a large monkey.

But, other people have also seen something. Or the tracks of something.

What about their reports?

Chapter Eight

Tracking the Snowcreature

The Himalayas are rugged mountains, difficult to reach from the outside world. Few people visit them today. There were even fewer visitors years ago.

The early visitors were not tourists. They were mountaineers who came to scale Mount Everest. Each wanted to be the first ever to reach the top of the world's highest mountain. Colonel Lawrence Waddell of England was among them.

Waddell started up Everest in 1887. He never got anywhere near the top. But he returned with a strange story. He had found some large footprints up there in the snow.

"I've never seen anything like them," he told his friends. "They were too big for a human foot —18 inches [46 cm] long. But they looked like a human foot. The toes were all set close together. The big toe was shaped like a thumb."

The Colonel wondered if he had come upon the prints of an animal unknown to the world.

A few years later, another climber reported seeing some prints. They were the same size as those sighted by Waddell. Once again, the toes were close together.

Then came the story of William Knight. He was from England and had tried to climb Everest in 1903. His story was even stranger than Waddell's. He said that he had actually stumbled upon a wild-looking creature.

On seeing the thing, Knight crouched behind a boulder. He studied the creature closely. It was pale yellow all over. A thatch of matted hair crowned its head. There was just a little hair on its face. The creature walked upright. It carried something that seemed to be a primitive bow.

"I watched it for five or six minutes," Knight

reported. "Then it moved off at great speed. It didn't see me the whole time."

More sightings came during the next few years. In 1923, a group of climbers stopped to gaze at a slope high above them. They could make out some dark figures that appeared to be much larger than human beings.

When the climbers reached the slope, the things were gone. But they had left some large footprints in the snow.

Next, an Italian explorer named A. N. Tombazi came down from Everest in 1926 with a report of a sighting. He said that the creature was walking upright. Now and again, it stopped to pull up a plant from the ground. It wore no clothing. Tombazi watched until it disappeared from view.

The world paid little attention to these reports. Most people believed that the climbers had been "seeing things." Or they agreed with what the scientists of the day were saying.

The scientists felt sure that the sightings had been of animals. The climbers had probably seen the red bear of the Himalayas. Or a very large langur monkey.

The mystery continued through the years. John Hunt of England found some tracks during a 1937 climb. Then, in 1948, the Norwegians ran into the two creatures that came right up to them. Slowly, some of the skeptics began to change their minds.

Perhaps, after all, there *was* some strange animal up there in the cold air. Perhaps there *was* a creature that was part human and part beast.

Perhaps there really *was* an Abominable Snowcreature.

A climber named Eric Shipton was greatly responsible for this new thinking. It happened while he was climbing Everest in 1951. He came upon some footprints on a glacier. He took out a camera and photographed them.

His pictures showed the footprints to be large ones. Each foot was about twice the size of a human foot. The big toe looked like a thumb. There was a wide space between it and the second toe. The second toe was even longer than the big toe.

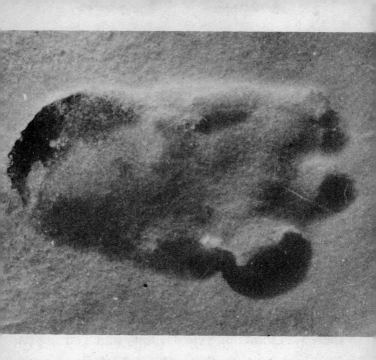

Note the odd shape of the toes on this footprint believed to have been made by an Abominable Snowcreature. This photograph was taken by Eric Shipton while he was climbing Mt. Everest in 1951.

It was bent to one side near the middle. The remaining toes were very small.

Shipton knew of all the earlier sightings. He had seen strange tracks himself back in 1936. But he had never really believed in the Snowcreature. Now he wondered.

So did many scientists. They looked at the pictures. They said that the prints weren't made by a bear or by any other animal they knew.

There was more news in 1953. In that year, Sir Edmund Hillary and Tenzing Norgay became the first men to reach the top of Everest. Word of their triumph was flashed around the world. And there was something else. Hillary and Tenzing had found some footprints while climbing. Strange, large footprints.

Made by an Abominable Snowcreature?

The Snowcreature now seemed to catch everyone's interest. People all across the world wanted to know if it really existed. They wanted to know what it really was. Several expeditions tried to find out in the next few years.

A newspaper in England sent out the first expedition. The leader was Ralph Izzard, a reporter. He hoped to capture a Yeti alive for study. Or, if that failed, he hoped at least to catch a picture of one. His search took him all through northern Nepal. It lasted for several months in 1954.

The reporter came home in disappointment. He didn't see a single Snowcreature. But he did photograph a lot of tracks. And he said that he had seen a Yeti scalp. He brought back several hairs from it.

Izzard found the scalp in a monastery high in the mountains. The Buddhist monks there said that the scalp was over 300 years old. It was shaped like a cone and covered with reddish hair. Izzard took some pictures of it. Then the monks allowed him to pluck out several hairs.

A study was made of the hairs. They proved to be a puzzle. No one could tell what kind of animal they came from.

Three American expeditions tried next, in 1957, 1958, and 1959. They brought back plaster casts of large footprints. But they found no Snowcreature to study. And they took no photographs.

Then Edmund Hillary stepped into the picture.

In 1960, he returned to the Himalayas. But this time he was not out to climb Everest. He was out to find the Snowcreature.

Hillary had conquered the highest mountain in the world. Would he now succeed at this?

Chapter Nine

The Mystery
Goes On

Hillary's search took him deep into the Himalayas.
He photographed some strange footprints along
the way. He stopped in villages and listened to
stories of the Yeti.

But he was deeply disappointed. Not once
did he see a Yeti for himself. Not once was he
able to snap a picture of the hulking creature.

He did feel excited, though, when he came at
last to the village of Khumjung. He had heard
stories that the people there had a Yeti scalp in
their possession. It was one of their great treasures.

Hillary wanted to see the scalp. In fact, he
hoped to borrow it. He planned to take it to the
United States for study. Surely, scientists would

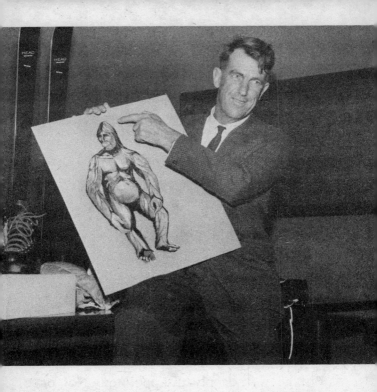

**Sir Edmund Hillary at a news conference
shortly before his 1960 expedition
to the Himalayas in search of the
Abominable Snowcreature.**

learn much from it. Much more than from the few hairs that Izzard had brought back.

The people of Khumjung gave Hillary a warm welcome. They knew of his great victory on Mount Everest. He asked to see the scalp. They brought it out and placed it before him.

It was very similar to the one Izzard had seen. Dome-shaped. Pointed at the top. Covered with thick hair. Black-and-red hair. The whole thing was somewhat larger than a human scalp. It could be worn like a hat and it would still be too big.

The villagers quickly shook their heads when Hillary asked to borrow the scalp. They didn't want it to leave their homeland. They were afraid.

"The gods will be angry with us," one explained, "if you fail to bring it back."

But Hillary slowly talked them into changing their minds. He told them how important it was to solve the mystery of the Yeti. He promised to return the scalp. He promised to give some money to the local monastery. And he promised to help build a school for the village children.

At last, the people of Khumjung agreed. But they insisted on one thing.

"You are our friend and we trust you. But one of our men must go with you. He will act as caretaker of the scalp. It will be his duty to see that no harm comes to it."

A few weeks later, Hillary and the "caretaker" arrived in the United States. Scientists in Chicago studied the scalp. Then it was sent to scientists in Paris.

The word that came back from them all disappointed Hillary. It made his whole trip seem a failure. The scientists said that the scalp was several hundred years old. But it didn't come from a strange creature. Rather, they thought it came from a bear or a serow—a goat antelope that is found in many parts of eastern Asia.

But one mystery surrounded the scalp. The scientists found parasites in it. These are tiny organisms that cling to living things and feed on them. Parasites, however, are not known to live on the serow or on the Himalayan bear.

Then why were they in the scalp?

The scientists didn't know the answer.

A disappointed Hillary returned the scalp to Khumjung. He knew that he hadn't solved the mystery of the Snowcreature. It remains a mystery to this day.

As in the past, many people today say there is no such thing as the Snowcreature. They start by pointing to the footprints.

"The prints are large, yes," they admit. "But they weren't that large to start with. They were made by a bear or a langur monkey. Or perhaps even by a human. Then the sun melted the snow. The tracks became larger. Finally, they looked as if they were made by a monster."

Or:

"Some Sherpas say that they've seen giant Snowcreatures. Others say they've seen Snowcreatures the size of young children. Bears are the giants. Langur monkeys the small ones. It's just as the scientists said years ago."

People who believe in the Snowcreature shake their heads at these arguments.

"Maybe the melting snow did make the tracks larger," they say. "But look at the tracks themselves. Look at their strange shape. They

(79)

came from something strange. It doesn't seem to be human or even any known animal."

They continue:

"The Snowcreature walks upright. Everyone who has seen it says this. And so it can't possibly be a bear or a monkey. They're four-legged animals. They can walk on their hind legs but only for a few steps at a time. The Snowcreature has been seen striding along for great distances."

One part of the Snowcreature mystery is especially puzzling. It seems to have some relatives in distant places.

There have been reports through the years of a human-like beast in Mongolia, which lies far to the north of Nepal. And there have long been many stories of a strange creature in South America.

There may also be a beast like the Snowcreature living on the West Coast of the United States. The Indians there say that their ancestors first saw this strange being centuries ago. They gave it the name "Sasquatch."

In recent years, a number of campers in California, Oregon, and Washington have caught sight of Sasquatch or its tracks. The tracks are gigantic. They've caused the newspapers to give it a second name—"Bigfoot."

Two campers sighted the thing in Northern California. The year was 1967. They were carrying a motion picture camera and managed to get some shots of it. The film showed a hairy creature about 7.5 feet (2.3 m) tall. It looked as if it weighed around 800 pounds (360 kg). It walked upright and took long strides as it walked through the woods.

It paused for a moment. It looked right at the camera. Then it disappeared behind the trees.

Experts checked the film. They said that it did not seem to be fake. But the film was quite blurred, so no one could really say what the creature was. An ape? An unknown animal? Or someone that the campers had dressed up in a furry costume as a hoax?

The stories of human-like animals in several parts of the world have caused some scientists to wonder. Is it possible, they ask, that these creatures are the last members of a family of apes that lived in prehistoric times?

If so, perhaps they are the "missing link"—

the connection that scientists have never been able to find between humans and their animal ancestors.

Not many people think that they are.

But perhaps we'll find out for certain one day.

Just as we may find out about those two other great puzzles—the Bermuda Triangle and the UFOs. When we do, we'll know much more about our world.

And about ourselves.

Index

Abominable snowcreature.
   See Yeti
Airplanes
   disappearances, 5–11,
      18–20, 23, 25–28
   UFO sightings and,
      41–43, 52–53
Antimatter, 27
Arnold, Kenneth, 33–34,
   39–40

Bermuda Triangle
   location, 11
   magnetic forces in, 28–
      29
   physical forces in, 23–
      27
Bigfoot. *See* Sasquatch

Burack, Dan, 11–12

Columbus, Christopher, 14–
   16, 27–28
Compasses, 14–15, 27–28

Dahama, La, 20, 25
Devil's Triangle. *See* Bermuda Triangle

Earthquakes, 25
Extraterrestrial life, 30, 37–
   40, 45–46, 53–55
Ezekiel, 35

Flying saucers. *See* UFO

Gernon, Bruce, 21, 29

Gulf Stream, 23–24

Hamilton, Alexander (fl. 1897), 36–38
Hill, Barney, 47
Hillary, Edmund, 65, 72, 74–79
Hunt, John, 70

Izzard, Ralph, 72–73

Knight, William, 68

Norgay, Tenzing, 65–66, 72

Planets, 53–54
Project Blue Book (U.S. Air Force), 41, 44–47

Quicksand, 24

St. Elmo's fire, 17
Sasquatch, 80–81
Sherpas, 61–66, 79
Shipton, Eric, 70–72
Solar system, 54
Somers, George, 16–17
Spaceships, 30, 34–35, 37–38, 55
Stars, 53–54
Stivers, George, 6–8

Talley, Joe, 17–18, 25

Taylor, Charles, 5–9, 28
Tidal waves, 25
Tombazi, A. N., 69
Tornadoes, 25

Unidentified flying objects. See UFO
UFO, 33–35
    definition of, 34, 41
    explanations for, 41–45, 53–55
    hoaxes, 44, 46
UFO sightings
    Caribbean, 44
    China, 35
    Egypt, 35
    France, 36, 38, 49–50
    Great Britain, 36, 50–51
    Greece, 38
    Germany, 38
    Iran, 52
    Japan, 36
    Korea, 49
    Mexico, 36
    Middle East, 35
    Switzerland, 48–49
    Turkey, 38
    United States, 33, 36–40, 47, 50, 52
    Vietnam, 48

Waddell, Lawrence, 67–68

Waterspouts, 25

Yeti
    description, 63–64, 68,
       70–72, 80
    physical evidence, 70,
       73, 75–79

See also
    Sasquatch
Yeti sightings
    Mongolia, 80
    Mt. Everest, 68–70
    Nepal, 59–61, 65–66
    South America, 80

Edward F. Dolan, Jr. has written more than forty books for young people and adults. He served in the 101st Airborne Division during World War II. Mr. Dolan has written for radio, television, newspapers and magazines, and has been a magazine editor. His most recent Franklin Watts books are *Gun Control: A Decision for Americans* and *Child Abuse*.

A native of California, he now lives just outside of San Francisco with his wife, Rose.

If you liked this book, here are some more great stories for you to read.

INCREDIBLE CRIMES by Linda Atkinson
Open this book and enter some of the most amazing crimes in history—including a man who received $200,000 in ransom parachuted out of a plane in a blinding snowstorm . . . and was never seen again. And a gang of small-time crooks who, after two years of planning, netted over a million dollars in fifteen minutes.

PSYCHIC STORIES STRANGE BUT TRUE by Linda Atkinson
Can people really read minds? See the future? Bend objects by just thinking about them? The stories in this book are certainly puzzling. Some are shocking. But can they be true? Read them and judge for yourself.

ONE DARK NIGHT by Wallace White
When 15-year-old Greg goes to visit his uncle, the sheriff of a small Southern town, he has no idea anything is wrong. But it soon becomes clear that trouble is brewing. And as Greg's worst suspicions are confirmed, a terrifying series of events thrusts him into a night of brutality in the darkness of an old quarry.

THE BERMUDA TRIANGLE AND OTHER MYSTERIES OF NATURE by Edward F. Dolan, Jr.
Mysterious disappearances in the Bermuda Triangle. The Abominable Snowman. UFOs. All incredible mysteries that have baffled authorities for decades. Are they science fiction or science fact? Read this book and decide.

Read all of these great books, available wherever Bantam Books are sold.

MS READ-a-thon—
a simple way
to start youngsters reading.

Boys and girls between 6 and 14 can join the MS READ-a-thon and help find a cure for Multiple Sclerosis by reading books. And they get two rewards — the enjoyment of reading, and the great feeling that comes from helping others.

Parents and educators: For complete information call your local MS chapter, or call toll-free (800) 243-6000. Or mail the coupon below.

Kids can help, too!